Little Tim
and the
Brave Sea Captain

by Edward Ardizzone

- To Philip from his father -

Frances Lincoln
Children's Books

Text and illustrations © Edward Ardizzone 1936

First published by Oxford University Press in 1936
This edition published in the UK in 2015 by Frances Lincoln Children's Books,

74–77 White Lion Street, London N1 9PF · www.franceslincoln.com

British Library Cataloguing in Publication Data available on request

ISBN: 978-1-84780-735-9

Printed in China

1 3 5 7 9 8 6 4 2

Little Tim lived in a house by the sea.

He wanted very much to be a sailor.

When it was fine he spent
the day on the beach playing
in and out of the boats, or
talking to his friend the old

boatman who taught him all about
the sea and ships.

Sometimes Tim astonished

his parents by saying, "That's a Cunarder," or "Look at that Barquentine on the port bow."

When it was wet Tim
would visit Captain McFee, who

would tell him about his voyages
and sometimes give him a sip of
his grog, which made Tim want to
be a sailor more than ever.

But alas for Tim's hopes. When he asked his mummy and his daddy if he could be a sailor they laughed and said he was much too young which made Tim very sad.

He was so sad that he resolved to run away to sea.

One day the old boatman told Tim that he was going out in his motor boat to a steamer which was anchored some way out. Would Tim like to come, too? Tim was overjoyed.

The boatman went on to say that the Captain of the steamer was a friend of his, and, as the steamer was about to sail, he wanted to say good-bye to him.

Tim helped the boatman to launch the boat and off they went.

Tim got more and more excited as
had never been

they neared the steamer as he
in one before.

When they arrived alongside they clambered on board. Tim was left on the deck while the boatman went to see the Captain who was in his cabin.

Now Tim had a great idea. He would hide and when the boatman left, not seeing Tim, he would forget all about him.

This is exactly what happened.

Off went the boatman and away went the steamer with Tim on board.

When Tim thought
that there was no chance
of being put on shore
he showed himself
to a sailor.

"Oi," said the
sailor." What are
you doing here?
Come along with me,
my lad. The Captain will
have something to say to
you."

When the Captain
saw Tim he was
furious, and said Tim
was a stowaway
and must be
made to work
his passage.
So they
gave Tim a pail

and a scrubbing
brush and made
him scrub the deck
which Tim found
very hard work. It
made his back ache
and his fingers sore.
He cried quite a lot
and wished he had never
run away to sea.

After what seemed hours
to Tim the sailor came
and said he could
stop work and
that he had not
done badly for
a lad of his size.
He then took Tim
to the galley where
the cook gave him
a mug of cocoa.

Tim felt better after the cocoa and when the sailor found him a bunk he climbed in and was soon fast asleep. He was so tired that he did not even bother to take off his clothes.

Tim soon got accustomed to life on board. As he was a bright boy, and always ready to make himself useful, it was not long before he became popular with the crew. Even the Captain said that he was not too bad for a stowaway.

Tim's best friend was the cook who was a family man. Tim would help him in the galley and in return get any nice titbits that were going.

Besides helping the cook Tim would run errands and do all sorts of odd jobs, such as taking the Captain his dinner and the second mate his grog,

helping the man at the wheel, and sewing buttons on the sailor's trousers.

One morning the wind started to blow hard and the sea became rough which made the steamer rock like anything. Poor Tim felt very sick and could not eat any of the titbits that the cook gave him.

All that day the wind blew harder and harder and the sea got rougher and rougher, till by night-

fall it was blowing a terrible gale.

In the middle of the night there was a fearful crash. The ship had struck a rock.

The sailors rushed on deck shouting, "We are sinking. To the boats. To the boats." With great difficulty they launched the boats and away they went in the raging sea.

— But —

—they had quite forgotten Tim. He was so small and frightened that nobody had noticed him. Tim crept onto the bridge where he found the Captain who had refused to leave the ship.

"Hullo, my lad," said the Captain. "Come, stop crying and be a brave boy. "We are bound for Davey Jones's locker, and tears won't help us now."

So Tim dried his eyes and tried not to be too frightened. He felt he would not mind going anywhere with the Captain, even to Davey Jones's locker.

They stood hand in hand waiting for the end.

Just as they were about to sink beneath the waves Tim gave a great cry. "We're saved. We're saved."

He had seen the lifeboat coming to rescue them.

The lifeboat came alongside
and a life line was thrown to them,
down which, first Tim, and then

the Captain were drawn to safety.

Hardly had they left the steamer when it sank beneath the waves.

When the lifeboat came into the
on the quay to watch its return gave a
Captain, and realized that the lifeboat had

harbour, the crowd which had gathered great cheer. They had seen Tim and the made a gallant rescue.

When the lifeboat docked, Tim was lifted out and he and the Captain were taken to the nearest house,

where they were
wrapped in blankets and
sat in front of the fire
with their feet in tubs
of hot water. Then
having got nice and
warm they were put to bed
where they slept
hours and hours.

The next morning
Tim sent a telegram
to his parents
saying that he
was taking the

train home and that the
Captain was coming too.
Then he and the
Captain, after thanking
the lifeboatmen and
the kind people who
had put them up,
went to the station
and caught their train.

Tim's parents were at the garden they arrived. Captain McFee and the boat- pleased Tim was to see his daddy and his

gate to give them a great welcome when man were there, too. You can imagine how mummy and his old friends again.

The Captain told
Tim's parents all
about their adventures
and how brave Tim had
been and he asked them if they would let
Tim come with him on his next voyage as he
felt that Tim had the makings of a fine sailor.

Tim was very pleased and happy to hear
his parents say yes.

The lifeboatmen were pleased, too, as they
were presented by the Mayor with medals for
bravery.

~ The End ~